Nathaniel Hawthorne, James Edgar Smith

The Scarlet Stigma

Nathaniel Hawthorne, James Edgar Smith

The Scarlet Stigma

ISBN/EAN: 9783337343408

Printed in Europe, USA, Canada, Australia, Japan

Cover: Foto ©Andreas Hilbeck / pixelio.de

More available books at **www.hansebooks.com**

The Scarlet Stigma

A Drama

In Four Acts

By

JAMES EDGAR SMITH.

Founded upon Nathaniel Hawthorne's Novel,
"The Scarlet Letter."

WASHINGTON, D. C.
JAMES J. CHAPMAN,
1899.

STIGMATIZATION is a rare incident of ecstasy. Not many well authenticated cases have been reported by competent medical authorities, and yet there can be no doubt of its occasional occurrence. See Encyclopaedia Britannica, article on Stigmatization by Dr. Macalister, and references therein cited; also the work on Nervous and Mental Diseases by Dr. Landon Carter Gray, page 511. That it may occur in men of a high order of ability is instanced by the case of St. Francis of Assisi.

It ought not to be necessary to point out that the entire third scene in the second act of this play is a dramatic transscript from the diseased consciousness of Mr. Dimsdell, that the Satan of the play is an hallucination, and that the impress of the stigma upon Dimsdell's breast is merely the culmination of his auto-hypnotic ecstasy, or trance.

PERSONS REPRESENTED.

ROGER PRYNNE, called *Chillingworth*, a physician.
ARTHUR DIMSDELL, a youthful divine.
JOHN WILSON, a good old minister.
BELLINGHAM, Governor of the Colony.
BUTTS, a sea captain.
SATAN, an hallucination of Dimsdell's.
BRONSON,
WARD,
LANGDON, } Members of the Governor's Council.
ARNOLD,
DIGGORY, a servant to Governor Bellingham.

HESTER PRYNNE, wife of Roger Prynne.
MARTHA WILSON, daughter of Rev. John Wilson.
URSULA, a nurse.
BETSEY, a milkmaid.
MOTHER CAREY, keeper of a sailor's inn.

A *Clerk*, a *Crier*, a *Jailer*, *Councilors*, *Citizens*, *Soldiers*, *Sailors*, *Indians*, *Servants*.

SCENE—*Boston*.   TIME—*June, 1668.*

THE SCARLET STIGMA.

ACT I.

SCENE I.—*A tavern and a street in front of it. Settles on porch.* SAILORS *smoking and drinking. Enter* CAPTAIN BUTTS, *singing.*

Butts. *The Margery D. was a trim little ship,*
    The men they could man, and the skipper could skip;
    She sailed from her haven one fine summer day,
    And she foundered at sea in the following way,—
        To-wit:
All. *A-rinkety, clinkety, clink, clank, clank,*
    The liquor they bathed in, the spirits they drank;
    A sailor at sea with three sheets in the wind
    Can hardly be called, sirs, quite sober.

Enter MOTHER CAREY, *from Tavern.*

Carey. Cap'n! Cap'n Butts! Gen'le gen'lemen! wou!d

ye rune a pore widdy woman by a singing of sech filthy
tunes?   And me up for my license again nex' Tuesday!

Butts. Peace!   Peace, Mother Carey, hear your chick-
ens screech!   Come, boys!   [*Singing.*

> *The captain was thirsty, and so was each man,*
> *They ladled the grog out by cup and by can,*
> *The night it was stormy, they knew not the place,*
> *And they sang as they sank the following grace,—*
> > *To-wit:*
>
> *All.   A-sinkety, sinkety, sink, sank, sunk,*
> *Our captain is tipsy, our mate is quite drunk,*
> *Our widows we leave to the world's tender care,*
> *And we don't give a damn for the Devil!*

Ha! Ha! Ha!

Carey. O, Lord!   O, Lord!   If the magistrates should hear
that song, they'd close my place!

Butts. There, there now.   [*Chucks her under the chin.*]
The magistrates are not as quick to hear a sailor sing as
thou art to take his orders.   Bring us a pint apiece.

Carey. Thou naughty man!   [*Slaps his jaws.*]   A pint
apiece?   [*Exit.*

Butts. Aye.   Now, lads, bargain out your time; ye'll
not see a petticoat for many a day.   [*Lights pipe and sits.*

Sailors. Aye, aye, sir.

CITIZENS *cross stage, singly and in groups, all going in the same
direction.   Enter* MOTHER CAREY *from house with ale, serves it,
looks up and down street as in expectation of some one, then goes in.*

Butts. Mother Carey's lost one of her chicks.   Here lads!

here's to the mousey Puritan lassies! They won't dance, they can't sing—Ah! well! here's to them till we come again! [*All drink.*

Enter along the street two COUNCILORS.

Arnold. 'Tis very true; but, sir, though many break this law and go unpunished, our godly Company should not wink at known adultery.

Langdon. In other words, we must find scape-goats to bear our sins.

Arnold. Nay, not exactly that. We vindicate God's laws, and—— [*Exeunt Councilors.*

Butts. He must be Privy Councilor to the Lord Himself!

Enter a group of WOMEN.

First Woman. Her beauty, say'st thou? Pretty is as pretty does, say I. I'd beauty her! Go to! Who knows the father'of her brat; can any tell?

Second Woman. Thou dost not doubt thy goodman?

First Woman. Trust none of them. I know mine own; dost thou know thine? As for her she hath shamed our sex, and I would— [*Exeunt Women.*

Butts. God's-my-life, there's more poison in their tongues than in a nest of rattlesnakes? What's all this pother, lads?

Sailor. There's a trial, sir, on a charge of bastardy.

Butts. Ha! ha! ha! You rogues had better ship elsewhere; if the wind sits in that quarter, you'll find foul weather here.

Sailors. Ha! ha! ha!

More people cross the stage.

Butts. Cheapside on a holiday!

Re-enter MOTHER CAREY, *dressed for walking.*

Carey. O, dear! O, dear! I'll be late; I'm sure I'll be late. Oh! dear, dear, dear! why will that Ursula still lag?

Butts. What's the matter, Mother?

Carey. Matter? Matter enough! a gentlewoman tried for adultery and me sure to miss it all! [*Looks around.*] Why doesn't Ursula come? O, dear! O, dear!—why, here she is!

Enter URSULA.

What kept thee, Ursula?

Ursula. Such a crowd! Whew! I'm out o' breath. [*Sits; one or two pass over.*] The town's run mad to look upon a gentlewoman shamed. [*Citizens still pass.*] Ah! there's no room for me now, but when her labor came God knows there was no press! I had room enough then, not one would lend a hand—fie! they are serpents, all of them; they have double tongues to hiss, but ne'er a hand to help.

Carey. Still talking to herself. Here, Ursula, take the keys and wait upon the gentlemen.

[*Hands keys to Ursula and exit up street.*

Ursula. Let the gentlemen wait on me awhile.

Butts. Would you have us die of thirst, Ursula?

Ursula. What will you have, Captain?

Butts. Stingo, Ursula, stingo!   [*Exit Ursula in tavern.*

What say you, lads, shall we see this trial?

Sailor. Aye, aye, sir, the woman's fair to look upon.

Butts. Then let us get our ballast in, hoist sail and tack away.

Re-enter URSULA *with ale.*

Who is it, Ursula, they try?

Ursula. A gentle lady, sir. God's-my-life, had no man tempted her—but, that's your ways, you tempt us, blame us when we yield, and then make laws to punish us.

Butts. But, what's her name?

Ursula. What should it be but Hester Prynne?

Butts. Hester Prynne? The gentle Mistress Prynne I brought from Amsterdam three years ago?

Ursula. The same, God bless her.

Butts. My lads, don't wait for me.   [*Exeunt Sailors.*

I knew her husband, Ursula; a man
Well versed in all the wisdom of the time;
Somewhat well gone in years, but lovable
Beyond the shallowness of youth, and rich
In mellow charity. Oft hath he sailed
With me from port to port where learning drew him,
And still came richer home. One day he shipped
For Amsterdam and brought his bride, who, like
A hawthorn in its pink of youth that blushes
'Neath the shadow of an ancient elm,
Shed spring-time sweetness round his green old age.
I've seen them often in their Holland home,
Where wisdom laid its treasures at the feet
Of love, and beauty crowned the offering.
She was a lovely lady, Ursula,
And when her lord, still bent on learning more,
Resolved to come out to America—

His own affairs then calling him to England—
He placed her in my care, intending soon
To follow her.   He did, but curséd fate!
His ship was lost—no one knows where!

   Ursula.   Alack
The day!   She had not sinned had he been here.

   Butts. But, didst thou know her, Ursula, as I
Have known her, wisely good and true, thou wouldst
Have wondered more.

   Ursula.   Know her, sir!   I nursed her!

   Butts. Thou, Ursula?

   Ursula.   None but I!

   Butts. Where were her friends?

   Ursula.   Where, but at home! Dear heart,
They shunned her like the plague—though if the truth
Were known, many that shun her now would keep
Her company perforce.   None came near
But pious Master Dimsdell, and even he
Came only out of duty to her soul;
He told me so.

   Butts.   The Reverend Master Dimsdell
And thou her only comforters?

   Ursula.   Nay,
The little bairn was her greatest comfort, sir.

   Butts. How doth she bear her trouble, Ursula?

   Ursula. Like a good woman, sir.

   Butts.   She yet is that!
But have you never learned her lover's name?

   Ursula. Nay, I never have.

   Butts.   'Tis strange that she

Should fall; and then endeavor to conceal
Her lover! Noble, wise and beautiful,
No other than a man of mark could win her!

Ursula. A three years widow, baby three months old,
A coward run-a-gate of a lover, sir—
Tell me, is there no exception made
By law for widows?

Butts.   None, of which I know.

Ursula. The law is hard indeed!

Butts.   I wonder if
A rough sea-dog like me might speak a word
For her?

Ursula. Aye, that you might! Go seek the good
Old Doctor Wilson, mercy dwells with him,
And he will aid you, sir.

Butts.   I'll go at once.

   [Exeunt severally, Butts up street, Ursula in tavern.

   Enter ROGER PRYNNE, *travel stained.*

Roger. We are not masters of our paths, although
Our wills do seem to guide our faltering steps:
Ship voyagers are we, and roam at will
Within the narrow confines of the deck,
But neither plot nor steer the destined course.
I may have passed her house—I'll ask my way
Here at the inn. Long live King Boniface!
What ho! some wine!

Ursula. [*Within*] Your patience, Captain, I'll be there
anon.

Roger. At your leisure, hostess; I've learned to wait. [*Sits.*

A bachelor at sixty, I found myself
Encumbered with a ward—nay, not that—
Enriched with female loveliness and grace
Bequeathed unto me by a dying friend.
Volition had no part in that, nor in
My sudden recrudescency of love.
I willed our marriage; but 'twas fate bestowed
The joys I long had fled.   Then came our life
In Amsterdam; each day so filled with bliss
It overflowed into the next, and days
Of joy grew into weeks and months of happiness—
Let me have wine, I say!
   Ursula. [*Within*] Coming, sir!
   Roger. Anon the traveling itch—was't fate or will—
Possessed my soul to see America,
And money matters calling me to London,
Where raged the plague, I sent my wife before me
To America with Captain Butts, then bound
For Boston.   Ah! well-a-day, the parting!—
I hurried up my business; fled London town;
Shipped for America; was wrecked far South;
Captured by Indians; escaping, wandered North
Until I found the white man's colonies;
And now footsore and old I've reached the place
I first intended.   What next, O, Fate?

Enter URSULA.

Good morrow, hostess.
   Ursula.   Good morrow, sir.   [*Surprised.*
   Roger.   Look not
Askance upon my way-worn clothes; there's gold

To pay my reckoning.   [*Throwing money down.*
   Ursula.   Your pardon, sir;
I marveled, sir, so fine a gentleman
Should be so travel-stained.   What will you have?
   Roger. Bring me a cup of sherris-sack.
   Ursula. [*Aside*] I knew he was a gentleman!   [*Exit.*
✓ *Roger.* How will my Hester greet me? Will she know me?
She never saw me with a beard, nor in
Such rags.   Perhaps she thinks me dead—
If so, the shock might kill her—Let me see—
Putative widows have before my time
Bought second husbands with their beauty, wealth,
Or wit—and she hath all.   'Tis probable—
And when the long-supposed defunct returned,
He found his amorous relict the bride
Of a bright-eyed youth!   What worse, ye harpy fates?
She may be dead! Oh! this is madness!
Sweet Heaven, let her live! and, if I find
Her married, I'll depart unknown to her
And bury in my heart's deep sepulchre
My widowed grief. Bah! I'm a fool!
This weakness comes from my long wandering!
Misfortunes, though we think we conquer them,
Ever pursue, hang on our rear, and give
Such rankling wounds as teach our souls to dread
What else may lie in wait invincible.
             Re-enter URSULA *with wine.*
   Ursula. I beg your pardon, sir.   I could not find the wine
at first.
   Roger. Why, how was that?

Ursula. I'm not the hostess, sir, she is away; I merely take her place till she comes back.

Roger. You fill it rarely.

Ursula. God bless thee, sir, I'm cook, nurse, or hostess, as people need me. Ursula Cook, Ursula Nurse, or Ursula Goodale, at your service, sir.

Roger. Ah, indeed, Ursula! Then I presume thou knowest many of the citizens?

Ursula. I know them everyone.

Roger. This wine is excellent. [*Drinking*] Dost know one Roger Prynne?

Ursula. The husband of our Hester Prynne?

Roger. The same. [*Aside*] Thank God, she lives.

Ursula. He's dead, sir, rest his soul, a more than thirty months ago.

Roger. Poor fellow! He was a friend of mine. Where did they bury him?

Ursula. His ship was wrecked, he had no burial.

Roger. Here's to his memory! You know his wife?

Ursula. Alas; I do, sweet lady!

Roger. And why alas? The loss of a husband is no great calamity in a colony. There can be no dearth here of husband-material, I fancy.

Ursula. Whence come you that you know so little of the doings here?

Roger. From the far South, where for two long years and more I've lived among the savages. What do you mean?

Ursula. I mean her trial by the magistrates.

Roger. Tried by magistrates? For what?

Ursula. Adultery.

Roger. Tried for adultery?

Ursula. Aye, sir, that she is.

Roger. It is a lie, a damned lie! Tried for adultery! A likely thing! So pure a woman! A purer creature never lived!

Ursula. Sir, you are her friend? You know her?

Roger. I am—I am her husband—her husband's friend. I knew her in Old England. Adultery! A pretty word! Who doth accuse her? Damned detractors!

Ursula. Her child.

Roger. Her what?

Ursula. Her child.

Roger. Hath Hester Prynne a child? Well, well; that is news indeed! God bless the little thing! it can't be quite as much as three years old; nay, not so old. Why, such a tot can give no testimony. I'll go to this trial; I may be able yet to aid her. Adultery! Bah!

Ursula. God bless your heart, sir.

Roger. Is't a boy or girl, how old?

Ursula. A girl and three months old.

Roger. Three months? Three years you mean.

Ursula. Three months, I said.

Roger. Thou dost not mean that Hester Prynne hath borne a child within the last two years?

Ursula. I do. [*Aside*] A strange man, truly. This news hath troubled him; but that's not strange, it troubles all her friends. He seemed glad enough she had a child, but when I said it was a girl it seemed to sting him. Well, well! God help the women; we are unwelcome when we come, abused while we stay, and driven hence with ill-usage.

Roger. Adulteress! That cannot be! There's some
Mistake, or some deceit in this. Her great
Nobility of heart would take upon
Herself another's wrong. I'll take an oath
The babe they say is hers she never bore!
Ursula. 'Tis surely hers, for I delivered her.
Roger. Hester! Hester! O, my God! My Hester!
Woman, didst thou say that she is married?
Ursula. Nay, I said she is a widow, sir.
Roger. Who is her paramour?
Ursula. I do not know. [*Busies herself removing tankards.*
Roger. [*Aside*] Now is my honored name dragged in the
    dust
By her to whom I did confide its keeping ;
And she herself, my cherished wife, upraised
Upon a pedestal of shameful guilt
For filthy mouths to spit their venom at.
Slowly now. Whatever haps I'll be
Cornelius Tacitus for the nonce, nor brave
My state with that true name which marks me out
As Publius Cornutus. I must have time to think.
[*To Ursula*] Get me more wine. Prepare a room for me.
Ursula. Aye, sir. [*Going.*]
Roger. Where is this trial held?
Ursula. Sir, at the Market place, three crossings up
The street and to the left.
Roger.   I thank thee. Go. [*Exit Ursula.*
Why was the banishment of tyrant fate
Annulled by vigorous will? and why should I,
For whom the jaws of death unhinged themselves,

Escape from shipwreck, war, and pestilence,
And here attain my journey's end at last,
But that such evil deaths were much too mild
To gratify the fury that pursues me!
I was reserved for this last ignominy
As in despite of human purposes ;
Robbed of mine honor where most I placed my trust
And reap this pain where most I sowed for peace.
Was it for this that I did marry her?
Was it for this I sent her here before me?
For this I nursed the holy purposes
Of wedded purity, o'ercame the shocks
Of human destiny, and held in check
The inward passions of the baser man?
For this—to be cornuted in mine age
And die a by-word?
My purposes! My purposes! O, God!
Our purposes are little nine-pins
Which fate's sure aim bowls down incessantly :
As fast as we can set them up, events
Roll down the narrow alleys of our lives,
Rumbling like distant thunder as they speed,
Till crash! our king-intent is down, and in
His fall share all his puny retinue!
She an adulteress! My Hester, whom
I cherished as my soul! How I loved her!
Forgotten, like the meat of yesterday,
Let it pass!
Henceforth, for me there's nothing on this side
Of Hell, but study of revenge on him

Who wrought her shame.   He must have used foul means,
For she was ever chaste in thought and deed.
Hell fiend !   Now, under an assuméd name,
I'll ferret out her lusty paramour ;
Contrive some means to deeply punish him,
And satisfy my fathomless revenge.   [*Exit.*

SCENE II.—*Another street.   Enter* REV. ARTHUR DIMS-
DELL, *alone.*

Dimsdell. 'Twould do no good.—The Governor is late,
Or I have missed him.—Confess ?—Disgrace for me ;
No help to her ; and all the blasphemies
That evil minds could cast on sacred calling
Would be my blame.   Whereas, I now can make
My pleas take on the color of mine office
And yet reflect on it a purer glow.—
Why comes he not ?—The path of righteousness,
Though straight, leads on thro' pleasant fields to Heaven,
Whereas the broad and easy road of sin
Splits in its downward way, and then the will
Stands at a halt which fork to take, though both
Lead on to Hell !   Now—why, here he comes !

Enter GOVERNOR, *attended.*

Governor. Nay, Dimsdell, plead no more; she must be tried.
I know what thou wouldst say, and like thee for it ;
But think, my friend, the law would mock itself
If pardon did precede the penalty.

Dimsdell. Our Lord did pardon one was taken in
The very act.   O, think of Him !

Governor.   Enough !

What! wouldst thou have our laws contemned
As feeble nets to catch the smaller fry
And let the great break through? I tell thee, sir,
Her wealth, her beauty, her hitherto fair fame,
Blacken her crime and make its punishment
A signal warning to the baser sort.

Dimsdell. Hath she not suffered pains and imprisonment?
Enough to answer all the decalogue?

Governor. I stand for law; and you, I think, do think
You stand for gospel.—Come, we tarry.—
Plead with the Council for the woman, and, while
I think her death were well deserved, I'll not
Oppose their mercy if you win it.
My hand upon it. [*Going.*

Dimsdell. If that she be condemned,
Suspend her sentence till her paramour
Be found; and let them die together.

Governor. Agreed. Come, we're late. [*Exeunt.*

SCENE III.—*The Market Place.—Church with Portico, L.
—A pillory on a raised Platform, R.—The* GOVERNOR *and*
COUNCIL *seated in portico.—A crowd of* TOWNSFOLK.

Governor. Now that our other business is dispatched,
Call Hester Prynne.

Wilson. Wise Governor, and you,
My brethren: dried as I am with age,
The tendrils of my heart are pliable;
Nor have the tangles of this thicket-world
So twisted all my grain as not to bend
Before another's misery. Wherefore,

I do beseech you, call her not.

    Governor.   Yet must

We try the woman, though we pity her;

And though the scion mercy grafts upon

The stock of justice, the stock is justice still.

    Wilson. I plead for justice! even-handed justice!

As blind and cold as death—but with a sword,

Sharp on one side to reach the woman's heart

And on the other keener for the man's!

You call the woman; where's her paramour?

    Governor.   We do not know.

    Wilson.   Then grant a stay to Hester

Till he's known.

    Governor.   Too late; nor were it good

To let the woman slap the face of law,

And not resent it quickly. Once again,

Call Hester Prynne. The man she may discover.

    Enter Rev. ARTHUR DIMSDELL *through crowd and goes to Portico.*

    Crier. Hester Prynne! Hester Prynne!   [*Exit.*

    Dimsdell. Most worthy Governor, I am like one

Who waking hears the village clock toll time,

Yet, having missed the first few strokes, the hour

He cannot tell: and so stand I and hear

Fair Hester called. Is it for trial, or

For punishment?

    Governor.   For both.

    Dimsdell. I am her pastor and I speak for her;

I would to God that I could plead " Not guilty,"

Or in her stead could offer up myself

To satisfy the law!

Crowd.　　　How good he is!

Dimsdell. Gentle and wise she is, grave councilors,
And with a modest meekness goes about
The daily duties of her household care;
Oh! I am sure no vulgar palate-bait
Did lure her to this shame, but some enticement
That took the form of higher nature did
Invest the hook.　For she is modesty
Itself.

Governor. Can modesty, then, fall like this?

Dimsdell. The modesty of woman is like the blush
Upon a tender rose; it is her treasure
And her ornament: you cannot touch it,
But it fades away; or breathe upon it,
But it loses perfume; or bring it to the light,
Unwilted.

Governor. True, but when the roses fade
We cast them forth, nor treasure them again.

Dimsdell. 'Tis thus I own; but we have higher teaching.
Our Lord, who knew temptation's mighty power,
Yet was himself without sin's damning stain,
Did pass upon a case like this.　" Let him ·
Who hath no sin first cast a stone at her."
And then He said, " Go, woman, sin no more."
Oh! wondrous grace that pardoned frailty
Which had not sunk to vice!

　　　Re-enter CRIER *with* HESTER PRYNNE.

Governor.　　　　Enough!　Here comes the woman.
Hester, thou art accused before this court

Of that which blushing virtue shrinks to name,
Adultery.

    Hester. I pray you spare me.

    Governor. Thou art the widow of a man of whom
Report spake only praise: no act of thine
Hath openly offended decency,
But that young life which draws its sustenance
From thy round breast avows thy hidden shame.

    Hester. Have mercy on the babe, O, God!

    Governor. That thou shouldst sin, and thereby, Hester, bring
Dishonor on the name thy spouse did give thee,
Is worse than in a meaner woman. If thou
Hast aught to say to mitigate the wrath
Of justice, speak. And, Hester, bear in mind
The penalty is death or banishment.

    Hester. I would not gloze my crime, nor do I know
How to address your worships.
Yet since you bid me I will plead my cause
As best I can.
That I have sinned is true; and well I know
Henceforth for me there's nothing left from all
My kind but scorn and hate.
For me hath life no charm to cheat my hope,
Or make me wish to linger here; yet I
While lives the child would shelter her, the one
Sweet flower that lovely grows above the soil
Of my most foul debasement.
Although the blossom of iniquity,
She takes no tint from whence she springs, but rather
Of the sky toward which she doth unfold.

Believe me, sirs,
But for my babe's dear love, I'd ask for death
To rid me quickly of my misery:
For love itself, dishonored in my being,
Turns all the gentle cords that bind affection
Into hard-knotted thongs to whip me hence.
Therefore, if I do plead for life, think not
I do beseech a favor for myself,
But rather, that I beg a lingering pain,
Than expiate in one quick-ending pang
The sum of all my loathéd wickedness.
Thus, for my tender babe, I ask my life,
And, for myself, I do implore you now,
Banish me not.
As for my crime, I have repented it
Most bitterly; yea, I've suffered anguish
From the very hour when, as the spring
Of nature dragged my anchors loose, the soft
Entreaty of a lover's sigh did blow
Concurrent with my tide, and swept me out
Into a troubled sea.
Now, battered on the rocks of hard opinions,
My most untimely wreck is quite complete;
Yet spare the hulk for that dear freight it bore.

    Governor.   Woman, I pity thee; now, while our laws
Are strict, yet may our mercy show itself
In staving off the penalty, if thou
Wilt aid us.

    Hester. Your mercy comes with hard condition;
For how can I, who stand here helpless,

Aid you who have all power?

   Governor. Tell us who is thy paramour?

   Hester. That I will not do.

   Governor. Thou art most obstinate. What say you now,
Grave councilors? Need we delay the sentence?

   Bronson. Quick to forgive and slow in condemnation,
Would be our wisest course in such a case.
The life she hath God gave; we should not take it;
Nor should we banish her, for she is useful,
And with her needle doth assist the poor.
There is provision in our law to fit
This crime when neither death nor banishment
Is proper. It is: [*Reading*] "Th' adulteress shall stand
Upon the pillory; and on her breast
Shall wear a scarlet letter A, to mark
Her criminal incontinence."

   Governor.   A good
Suggestion truly; we had forgot the clause
From long disuse. What say you?

   Ward. I think it wise.

   Arnold.   'Twill be more merciful.

   Langdon. A living warning 'gainst adultery.

   All. It is our suffrage.

   Governor.   So be it then.
Hester, thou art to stand upon the pillory
A little while, and wear upon thy breast
The Scarlet Letter "A" forever;
This see thou do on pain of instant death
Or banishment. Hath anyone a piece
Of scarlet cloth?

Bronson. I have the letter here prepared.

Governor. Clerk, affix the letter to her breast.

Enter ROGER PRYNNE, *clad as in Scene I.—He keeps to the rear of Hester.*

Now, Jailer, lead her to the pillory,
There let her stand unbound.

Hester ascends steps to pillory platform.

Dimsdell, you are her pastor, speak to her.
Hold up her sin before her eyes, and warn
The multitude by her example.

    Dimsdell. I beg you, sir, let Dr. Wilson speak.

    Wilson. Nay, Dimsdell. Nay, the charge is yours.
Speak on. And plead that she disclose the man
Who was her paramour.

    Dimsdell. I pray you pardon me. I am not well.

    Governor. Not well? 'Tis but compassion weakens thee.
Speak man! thy words are gentlest and will draw
Her secret from her, though ours do seal her lips.
Proceed, Dimsdell.

    Dimsdell. We wrong her nature when we seek to know
That which her heart doth teach her to conceal;
Yet at your bidding will I plead with her.

Goes over to pillory.

Hester, look down upon me; let thine ear
Receive my meaning with the sound I make;
Behold in me the body of the Council,
Not me alone; and hear my words as though
The general voice, speaking in concert true,

Did intone them.
For it were vain presumption to expec t
That, what the Governor could not extract,
My words alone could move thee to disclose.

   Roger. A modest gentleman, truly !

   Dimsdell. Upon thy sin I dwell not; the penalty
Which thou dost suffer preaches repentance ;
And in thy nature there is naught to lead thee
Twice astray.
There's not an eye that now doth look upon thee
But pities thee, and doubt thou not, if he
Who wronged thee is present here, his heart is wrung
With bitterest remorse.   Wilt speak his name?

   Hester. I will not.

   Dimsdell. I do command thee by the Commonwealth,
I do entreat thee for thy reputation,
I do implore thee for thy soul's salvation,
Give up his name.

   Hester. I would not breathe his name to anyone ;
Nay, not to him who was my husband, though
The sea should cast him up to question me.

   Roger. Woman, who did seduce thee?

   Hester.   I keep my vow.

   Dimsdell. Hester, deceive thyself no more; look down
Upon me once again.   Believe me, Hester,
No pain the world could now inflict would harm
Thy recreant lover.   To see thee here set up
The target of a thousand curious eyes,
Thy beauties blistered in the noonday sun,
Thy gentle breast seared with yon scarlet letter,

Would burn that image on his soul.   Have mercy,
Hester, forgive his cowardice, do thou
Act for him ; pronounce his name and let him die
To satisfy his crime.

   Hester. I will not drag him down with me.

   Roger. Oh ! glorious generosity misplaced !

   Dimsdell. Your generosity hath led you once
Astray ; do not allow it now to aid
Him in hypocrisy.   For, Hester, you,
Who know his weaknesses and aspirations,
His station in his calling, his place in life
Among us, will be a party to deception
If now you hide his name.

   Hester. I answer to my God.   No man shall know
That which is only known to me and him.
But speak thou on his crime !

   Dimsdell. Ho ! all ye people of the commonwealth !
Behold !—let him confess !—O, Hester ! speak !—
I see--no more—   *[Dimsdell falls.*

Throng, confused and amazed, closes around Dimsdell.

Cries of horror and apprehension.

   Governor. Look to our brother Dimsdell.   He faints ;
The heat hath overcome him.

   Roger.   I am a doctor.   Make room !
The falling sickness.   Give us breathing space !

   Governor. Hester, thou art discharged.   Let all go home !
                                  [Exeunt.

ACT II.

SCENE I.—*Interior of Hester's home. Furniture Dutch-English, comfortable and handsome. Windows draped in scarlet-fringed curtains with scarlet cross-cords, simulating the letter "A." Rich needle work in the hangings and other accessories. A cradle L., near it a table with a quarto Bible.* HESTER *discovered bending over cradle, then sits R. C. and takes up a piece of embroidery (the letter "A" in scarlet on a dark background).*

Hester. God bless the little darling, how she sleeps!
Had I but thought that all my heart would beat
Within the tender compass of her arms,
I had not prayed she might not be. But now,
Although unasked she came, unasked she brought
A wealth of love and blessing to my soul.

       [Sits and embroiders.]

Thus Providence, although it pierce the heart,
Works into it some glorious design;
Which on this under side of life is blurred,
Thread over thread in infinite confusion.
Or, if we are not made of firmest texture,
The work pulls through, or tears an ugly rent,
Or gathers up our woof in meshy tangles.
This is a world of worn and fretted ends,

Knit in a maze of fearful intricacy,
Wherein we see no meaning. Nor can we know
The hidden shuttles of Eternity,
That weave the endless web of living, loving,
And begetting, whereby a filament
Of earth takes on the likeness of an angel.
The primal burden of our race-existence,
Mankind's perpetual perpetuation,
Weighs on weak womanhood; we bear the race
And all its natural ills, yet still our fellows,
Who proudly call themselves our lords and masters,
Do heap upon us petty wrongs, and load
Us down with their oppressions. I cannot tell
What rich reward my suffering may bring,
But bide the piercing, like this patient cloth,
In hope the needle carries golden thread.

       Enter a Maid-Servant.

What is it?
  Servant. Madam, a gentleman would speak with you.
  Hester. Bid him enter.   [*Exit Servant.*
Methought I heard my husband's dreaded voice
Speak to me on the pillory. What
If he lives, or hath arisen from the dead
To reckon with me now? Well, let him come;
For this strong heart outcast from sympathy
Hath turned back on itself in double strength;
And all the puny woman of my mind,
Burned in the furnace of my sex's scorn,
Plunged in the icy vat of love's neglect,
Hath tempered hard. I fear him not.

Enter ROGER PRYNNE, *shaved, and dressed as a
doctor of medicine.*

Roger himself!

Roger. Thou didst provide snug quarters, Hester, against
my coming. Aye, and hast furnished them better than I
bade thee.

Hester. The cost was small; my needle and my energy—

Roger. Have done the work; yea, and supplied the cradle
also. Ah! 'tis a brave piece of work; very beautiful and
delicate; the lusty offspring of lustful parents. Somewhat
costly, I should think, and asked some pains. Methinks,
thou hadst some help with that; or was it thy needle or thy
energy which wrought this dainty bit?

Hester. Touch not the child; 'tis mine, thou hast no part
in it.

Roger. Too true. But calm thyself. I have not harmed
the brat, nor did I touch it. [*Looking around.*] I like thy
taste, Hester. A handsome house to hold a handsome
woman.

Hester. The house is thine; let me and my babe depart.

Roger. Nay, keep the house, 'twill shelter you; I do not
need it.

Hester. I will not have it.

Roger. Will not, Madam Hester, is a strong word to use
to your wedded lord and master. I say you shall; yea, and,
furthermore, here is provision for the child and thee.

[*Throwing purse upon the table.*]

Hester. Take up thy purse. I who have done thee wrong
will not henceforth eat thy bread.

Roger. Wrong, Hester. Done me wrong? Wronged me?

Nay, Hester, wronged thyself; wronged thine innocent
babe; wronged the world; wronged whom thou wilt, but
not wronged me! To wake me from a doting dream—that
was not wrong! A dream of woman's purity and innocence; a foolish dream of married happiness between thy
youth and my decrepitude; to put an end to such a madness, surely was not wrong! Wronged me? Thy levity
hath righted my poor mind, which, pondering o'er thy beauties, listed to one side.

Hester. Oh! pardon me! ·

Roger. Pardon thee? yea, why should I not? I do pardon
thee; yea, more, I do applaud thine act. Thou wast no
slothful servant; thou didst not fear the coming of thy lord;
thou puttest all to use and gottest cent per cent. Therefore,
the care I show for thee is hire and wages; it is thy due,
accept it freely.

Hester. Let me and my babe depart. Receive thy money
and thy house, I can take nothing from thee. Ah! if I could
I would return thee every penny I have spent of thine.

Roger. Wait till I ask thee to account. What! am I so
old, and yet not know the cost of dalliance? Nothing
dearer. And he who eared my field during my absence,
being now, in thy abasement, so chary of his presence, spent
little of his gold, I'll warrant. Who is he, Hester?

Hester. Thou shalt never know.

Roger. Never's a long word, Hester; it stretches beyond
the judgment into eternity. Come, I'll know him then,
tell me now.

Hester. He is a scholar and can cope with thee; thou canst
not find him.

Roger. If he do walk the earth, I'll find him out ; if he be now in Hell, I'll follow him; where'er he be, his peace is forfeited and I will—

Hester. What wilt thou do to him?

Roger. Nothing, Hester, nothing. I merely wish to thank him for the love he showed thee during my absence, whereby thou didst mourn for me the less.

Hester. Thou wilt not kill him?

Roger. What a silly thing thou hast become, now thou hast left the path of virtue! Do I kill thee? Am I dangerous? Is there force in this withered body to harm a lusty knave, a brave seducer of ripe womanhood?

Hester. Nay, do not harm him.

Roger. At thy request, mistress.

Hester. The fault was mine.

Roger. No doubt 'twas thine alone.

Hester. Wreak vengeance then on me alone.

Roger. I have none.

Hester. I would I could believe thee.

Roger. As well give faith to me as him. But, truly, Hester, I had thought these puritans, these pilgrim fathers, had left all fleshly lusts behind them with their vanities in England. He must be a rare bird in these parts—O, I shall know him by his plumage!

Hester. He's safe enough.

Roger. Perhaps, but then these poachers, who fish in others' ponds, are proud of their achievements. They will talk. They brag in their cups and strut and ogle when they're sober.

Hester. I'll warn him of thee.

Roger. Thou wilt do nothing of the kind. But come,
Hester, man and wife ought not to quarrel. Let us set a good
example to the world in peace if not in chastity. Sit you
here and listen to me.

Hester. Well?

Roger. Hester, I loved thee when thou wast a babe,
A prattling child no taller than my knee,
A pretty little innocent, a tot
That wavered in its walk and won my heart
By tender trustfulness. Thou 'dt leave thy father,
Mother, all, to nestle in these arms
The whiles I told some worn out fairy tale,
Or sang of Robin Hood.
That was before thy mind did take its shape,
And subsequent events have blotted out
All memories of thy babyhood.

Hester. Nay, but I do recall, as in a haze,
Some of the incidents of infancy.

Roger. Perhaps. Hester, thou wast the dearest child
That ever blest fond parents, unfolding sweet
Thy mother's beauties and thy father's strength.
And canst thou now remember who made himself
A child to play with thee vain, foolish games;
Who taught thee out of books such lessons as
Thy little mind could grasp?

Hester. It was thou.

Roger. Then, as thou didst grow toward womanhood,
Some fifteen springs, thy gentle mother died;
A woman beautiful and pure, as sweetly
Ignorant of all her charms as is
The hyacinth.

Hester.   Mother! Mother!

Roger. Pray God the saints see nothing here on earth:
Or else that in their golden paradise
Some sleepy potion dull their sympathies
With us: for who could look upon this world,
And see mankind divested of the lies
That make our comeliness; or, with an eye undimmed,
Behold the brutal tragedies of life;
And yet find happiness or peace in Heaven?
Hell's flames would reach unto the tree of life
Itself and singe thy mother's heart, if she
Could see that scarlet letter on thy breast.

   [*Hester covers her face and moans.*]

Great God! what thread of continuity
Doth string the whirling incidents of life?
This woman was that maid whose purity
Excelled imagination's greatest reach;
Whose happiness sang ever like the lark
Arising from the earth to soar in Heaven!
And now behold her dyed in scarlet sin,
Branded with infamy, and moaning here
In deepest anguish!
Nay, come; let out thy grief in linkéd words,
For this tooth-gated dumb remorse will herd
Thy thoughts until they gore each other.
Hester, thy strength is greater than to yield
Thus to thy misery; do not lash
Thy heart into a fury; never blow
The tiny sparks of pain
Into the flaming coals of Hell.

That sinning soul is traitor to itself
That leagues its bruiséd thoughts with imps of Hell
To torture conscience.

Hester. Leave me, I pray you.

Roger. Not yet, else were my visit bootless.
Hester, I will not dwell upon thy life
From year to year, nor drag thy colliered soul
Back to its days of spotless innocence.
Thy father's amity for me, thou knowest,
And how, upon his death, I stood toward thee
In place of parents.

Hester. Would you had remained a father to me!

Roger. I loved thee, Hester; daughter, sister, sweetheart,
You were to me. And you did love me too,
And as an elder brother looked on me
In gentle confidence.
So did the years post by in th' dim afterglow
That comes to agéd men; while love with thee
Was in the dawning; a tender sky with both
Of us, my sun already set ; and thine
Not yet arisen; nor did it ever rise
To shine on me, fool that I was!

Hester. I never loved you, should not have married you;
Knew nothing then of love except the name.

Roger. Aye, you loved me, and you loved me not;
Hester, I wronged thee when I married thee;
The fault was mine, old as I was, to hope
To still the sweet necessities of youth
With passionless love; nature demands her due,
And we should know, while love may grow at home,

Passion requires some novelty.

Hester. We both have done foul wrong unto each other,
And, as this world doth judge, mine is the greater.

Roger. Yet thou wast tempted by thy youth, my absence,
A handsome lover's importunity:
But what can be said for me, old as I was,
To drive and badger thy chaste ignorance
To marry mine infirmities?

Hester. How can I right this wrong?

Roger. And wouldst thou if thou couldst?

Hester. Aye, if I could; but yet these broken lives,
Cracked by my fall, no putty will make whole.

Roger. Yet canst thou veil my ruin, and o'er me hang
The drapery of silence. Dost consent?

Hester. Aye, but how?

Roger. But swear to me thou wilt conceal my name,
Nor ever claim relationship with me,
Until I bid thee.

Hester.   Wherefore the vow?

Roger. Because I wish it;
Perhaps, because I would not bear the scorn,
The petty taunts, the contumelious looks,
That ever greet the cuckold husband.

Hester. Then will I take the oath.

Roger. Swear by the book, and also by the babe,
Never to breathe my rightful name;
Never to claim me as thy husband;
Never to leave this place.

Hester. Wherefore not leave the place?

Roger. Swear, woman, swear!

Never to leave this place, until I bid thee.

   Hester. I swear to all these things.

   Roger. Swear once again; never to tell thy paramour
Thy husband lives and walks these streets.

   Hester. I swear to keep thy counsel as I have kept
His and mine own.

   Roger. Remember then, from this time on, my name
Is Chillingworth, no longer Prynne, for that
I will not bear. [*Going*] Hester, farewell.
Yet ere I go, Hester, behold my mind:
I love thee still; but with a chastened heart
Made wise by sorrow. Day after day, as thou
Dost wend thy way about this mazy world,
My care will shield thee and thy little babe.
Do not repulse it. I have no hope that thou
Wilt think of me without revulsion;
Then hate me if thou must; but spare the thought
That ever thou didst take my hateful kisses,
Or clasp those soft warm arms about my thin,
Cold carcass.
Do not despise thy beauties that I once
Did own them. Forget it, Hester, for such a marriage
Was my infamy, and I it was
Who sinned against thy youth. Farewell!   [*Exit.*

   SCENE II.—*A Churchyard. A bell ringing for service.
Groups of people standing about. Persons cross stage and enter
church door on extreme L.*

   Bronson. They say the Reverend Master Dimsdell hath
Recovered from his fainting fit, and will,

God willing, preach to us this afternoon.

   Langdon. Aye, that he will.

   Arnold.   But hath he come?

   Ward.   Not yet;
He's late, but, whether here or elsewhere,
He's always doing good.

   Bronson.   A kindly man!
His feet do tread th' o'ergrown path that leads
Unto the poor man's door.

   Langdon.   Aye, that they do!
And, in the darkened hour of mortal grief,
His presence like a lamp gives light and hope.

   Arnold. His charity exceeds all human bounds,
And, though he's blameless in himself, knows how
To pardon others.

   Ward.   Aye, that he doth! Didst note
His plea for Hester Prynne upon her trial?

   Langdon. Aye, that I did!

   Ward.   But know the goodness of it!
He was her constant friend up to the time
Her wantonness declared itself, and then
He left her lonely, as though that punishment
Were all a man of mercy could inflict.

   Arnold. He takes it much to heart that wanton vice
Hath found a nest within his congregation.

   Langdon. That grief is truly great with him; but yet
He will not hear a word against her.—Look!
For here she comes.
How bravely doth she wear her scarlet letter!

Enter HESTER PRYNNE *alone; walks proudly, with slow steps, to porch and enters church; looking neither to the right nor to the left, but straight before her, with her head up. People turn to look at her, but no one speaks.*

First Woman. The brazen thing!

Second Woman. Didst note the fashion of her badge of vice, And how she's turned it into ornament?

Third Woman. A handy woman with her needle.

First Woman. Let's in and stare her out of countenance.

                                 [Exeunt Women.

Enter GOVERNOR BELLINGHAM *and* ROGER PRYNNE, *called Doctor Chillingworth.*

Governor. Now, as I told you, there hath lately come, But how I know not, a change in him so rare, It baffles cure.

Roger.   I think you said he is A very studious man?

Governor.   Aye, that he is. Good evening, gentlemen.

All.   Your worship.

Roger.   I pray you, tell me more.

Governor.   Nay, use your eyes, For here he is.

Enter REV. ARTHUR DIMSDELL. *People uncover as he passes. He salutes them gravely and generally.*

              Dimsdell, a word with you.

Dimsdell. Good evening, gentlemen.

Governor. Dimsdell, here is good Doctor Chillingworth, Who tended thee. I hope you gentlemen

Will prize each other at your native worths.

Dimsdell. I shall be glad to know you better, Doctor.

Roger. And I, to see you better, sir.

Dimsdell. Pardon me, I must in; I'm late already.

*Exit Dimsdell—all follow except Governor Bellingham and
Roger Prynne. Bell ceases.*

Governor. How weak a hold we have on health! That man
Is but the standing ruin of his former self,
And yet, for beauty, comeliness and grace,
He still is model to the colony.
What do you think, can care restore him yet,
And give him to us as he used to be?

Roger. I cannot tell. I need more knowledge of him.
There are no marks of cureless malady—
A faint suggestion of overwatchfulness,
That oft points out the student—nothing more.

Hymn from church. (*Tune:* "Ein' feste Burg" *or other
ancient hymn used by the Puritans.*)

Governor. The worship hath begun; but, ere we in,
A word about the wealth you left with me.

Roger. No more. Pray use it as your own, in trade,
Or howsoe'er you choose. The largest pearl
An Indian chief did give me; but sell it with
The rest, and with their worth provide for Hester.
She is the widow of mine ancient friend,
To whom I ever shall be much indebted,
And while I would not have her know me yet
As what I am—her husband's friend and hers—
As that might breed more grief in her, or wake

An old one—yet I think it meet to care
For her and for her child.
    Governor.   Your goodness is
Your passport, Doctor. Come, let us in.—Nay,
After you; you are my guest.   [*Exeunt.*

    SCENE III.—*Bed room of the* REV. ARTHUR DIMSDELL.
Night. DIMSDELL, *alone in the dark.*

    Dimsdell. O, she is beautiful!
The memory of her loveliness
Pervades my waking dreams, and, pleasant theft,
Deprives my sleep of dark oblivion.
And thus, while fleeing from the gentle bonds
Of love, I am become the thrall of passion,
And sigh my heart away in waste desire!
Had I but truly loved her,
Would not our joys, that then were innocent,
Have moulded soul to soul and made mine take
The form of her most dear perfections?
But, now!
No trait of Hester's noble purity
Remains with guilty me, for I purloined
Her precious diadem and like a rogue
I cast that crown away, afraid to wear
What would have been my dearest ornament.
Why can I not repent? Or is it true
Repentance is denied the hypocrite?
And must it then forever be that, though
I cast out sin, both root and branch, the seed
Of evil, scattered long ago, will sprout

And bloom carnation thoughts that dull the soul
With subtle sweetness!
Oh! coward that I am!
Bound down, as to a rock, to form and place,
By iron chains of worldly precedent,
While my desires like eagles tear my breast,
And make of me a base Prometheus.
O, God!
I married all the family of sins,
When I espoused the pleasantest; I am
Become a liar through my lechery,
A thief of reputation through my cowardice,
And—puh! the rest but follow in the train
Of my dear wedded crime!
O, God! and shall this lust burn on in me
Still unconsumed?   Can flagellation, fasting,
Nor fervent prayer itself, not cleanse my soul
From its fond doting on her comeliness?
Oh! heaven! is there no way for me to jump
My middle age and plunge this burning heart
Into the icy flood of cold decay?
None?   O, wretched state of luxury!
This hot desire grows even in its death
And from its ashes doth arise full fledged
Renewed eternally!

A blinding flash of lightning, followed quickly by sharp thunder,
    discloses Dimsdell kneeling at his couch, and also
        shows SATAN—*an archangel with bat*
            wings—who has just entered.

Have mercy upon me, O, my God, have mercy!

According to thy gentle lovingkindness,
According to the multitude of all
Thy tender mercies, blot out my foul transgression.
Purge me with hyssop, and I shall be clean;
Wash me, and I shall be whiter than snow;
Hide thy face from my sins, and blot out
All mine iniquities.

    Satan. You mar the psalm, Sir priest, for you omit
The saving clause.   Your sin is unconfessed.

    Dimsdell. Who art thou that durst interpose between
My soul and God?

    Satan. I am the stronger part of lower nature,
The worser part of all that came from Him
Whom all adore.   Behold me!

    Satan becomes visible by light emanating from himself.

    Dimsdell. Thou art Satan!   The Prince of Hell!

    Satan. I am so called.

    Dimsdell. Get thee hence!   I am a minister
Of God, a priest, and am anointed of the Lord
To teach His children.

    Satan. And, therefore, am I come to thee, Sir priest.
I do confess a predilection for
Thy calling; conclaves, synods, convocations,
Are never held without my guiding presence;
They are my field days and my exercises,
While in the study and the cell I take
My cloistered ease.   I love all priests and am
The bosom friend of many who would blush
To speak to me in public.   Receive me, brother.

Dimsdell. Scorner, avaunt!   Sink to the hell from whence
Thou cam'st!   I do abhor thee, Satan; yea,
I tell thee to thy face that I who quail
Before the awful majesty of God,
And cowardly do hide my sin from man,
I tell thee, vile as I am, I do detest
Thy very name!   I do defy thee!

Satan. These words are very brave; if more than wind,
Go to the market place tomorrow, there
Proclaim thy vice; or else ascend thy pulpit
And denounce thyself as what thou art, adulterer.

Dimsdell. Recreant to my God am I; think'st thou
That I will thee obey, to whom I owe
No deep allegiance?

Satan. Then bare thy sinful breast, for here I swear,
By that dread Name which mortals cannot hear,
I will upon thee print a mark, the stigma
Of thy secret crime.

Dimsdell. Hold off!   I charge thee by that other Name
Of Him who rent thy kingdom, and will destroy it,
Touch me not yet!
Almighty Purity, Dread Essence Increate;
Behold concentrate, in this wicked form,
The universal spirit of iniquity.
Come quickly in thy majesty, O Lord!
Wither him here within the awful flame
Of Thy bright Holiness!   Shrivel his frame
Into an atom, and blow the lifeless dust
Beyond the farthest star.
And, if in his destruction my soul should share

Through close proximity, spare not!
Then will Thy servants serve Thee, Gracious Lord!
And mankind find its paradise!
   Satan. That was well said!
Perhaps, Sir priest, you now will treat me to
A learned disquisition on the birth
Of evil? I'd like to hear it, if it tread
Beyond theology's well beaten path;
But, if it stumbles in the pug-mill round
Of teleology, you must excuse me.
   Dimsdell. Base siege of scorn! I curse thee!
   Satan. Curses but belch foul wind, they pass beyond me.
But, come; I have no time to waste with thee;
This visitation had not been, nor would
I dignify thy carnal slip by my
Incarnate presence, but for thy perfidy.
For thou hast reached a depth of moral baseness
Below the meanest fiend in lowest hell;
Thou hast deserted her who sinned with thee,
Gave up her virtue to express her love,
Laid down her treasure to thy secret lust,
And then took up thy burden with her own.
Think not I come to draft thee of my legions,
I would not have so weak, so mean a coward,
To sow pale fear among them. No!
Thou wilt be damned outside of Hell. I come
To show, as in a mirror, what thou art;
Not what thou shalt be. The past and present both
Are mine, the future rests with God. But now,
   Hester's image appears in a cloud dressed in white.

Behold the woman as thou first didst know her,
A loveliness to tempt or saint or devil,
The rare quintessence of pure womanhood !
Transparent brightness !   A living crystal globe,
Wherein all beauties of humanity
Reflect themselves with iridescent glow !
Dost thou remember ?
Behold her now the mother of thy babe,

The image of Hester changes.   She holds their babe
in her arms.

Whose pretty wiles would win hard Moloch's heart ;
Make him forget his rites, and turn man-nurse.
O, fool ! I would renounce my war with Heaven,
Eat up my pains in one most bitter mouthful,
And sue for pardon from God's hated Throne,
If such an offspring might but call me father !
Where is thy manly pride ?
But, now, behold her shamed, bearing the badge

Hester's image wears Scarlet Letter "A."

Of thy foul infamy.   Tear wide thy shirt,
For as thou look'st on her I will impress
Upon thy breast a stigma worse than hers.
Aye, fall upon thy knees to worship her
The Lady of the Scarlet Letter.
Yet while thou kneel'st thy flesh doth glow and burn

Scarlet Letter "A" glows on Dimsdell's breast.

With all the deep red heraldry befits
A coward lust : the latter "A" in gules

Upon thy sable heart.   There let it gnaw
Forever and forever!

> *Hester vanishes.   Satan fades.   No light, save "A" on*
> *Dimsdell's breast.*

And, now I go, I put this curse upon thee:
Be coward still, wear outwardly the garb
Of righteousness, shake in thy pious shoes,
Cover the stigma on thy breast from eyes
Of flesh, and be a hypocrite, till death
Relieves the world of thee.   We'll meet again.

> [*Lightning.   Exit Satan.   Dimsdell lies in trance.*
> *Night.   No sound, no light.*

Act III.

SCENE 1.—*The garden of Governor Bellingham.* ROGER
PRYNNE, *called Chillingworth, alone.*

Roger. The fox that robbed my roost is sly; he keeps
The cover warily; and, now the scent
Is cold, the curs that yelp in scandal's pack
Bay loud on many faults, but cannot trace him.

Enter DIGGORY.

Diggory. Doctor, the Governor will join you presently.
Roger. Diggory, I will await him patiently.   [*Sits.*
            Diggory retires, then returns.
Diggory. Doctor, may I beg a word with you?
Roger. A thousand if you will.
Diggory. I would speak in confidence.
Roger. The manner would become thee, Diggory.
But speak, man! Say on.
Diggory. I need a philter, Doctor. For the love of mercy—
Roger. For the love of good liquor, Diggory, thou shalt
have twenty filters. Still decanting?
Diggory. O, sir! not that kind of filter. I'm in love!
Roger. Ah! thou art in love? In love didst thou say?
Diggory. Aye, sir, if it please you.
Roger. It pleases me well enough; how doth it please the
lady?

Diggory. She's not a lady, sir, thank God! she's but a simple maiden, and it pleaseth her not.

Roger. A simple maid refuses you! Ah! Diggory, Diggory, be thankful for the good things God hath sent thee.

Diggory. Truly, sir, I thank Him ev'ry day; but, sir, as I do desire the maiden—I—I—would have her too.

Roger. And so, Diggory, thou wouldst have me aid thee in this folly, and give thee a love potion?

Diggory. Aye, sir, begging your honor's pardon.

Roger. But why dost thou ask me, Diggory? Dost thou take me for an herb-doctor, or a necromancer, or what?

Diggory. My master, the Governor, says you are a very learned man, a what-you-call-'em—a scientist; and a scientist can do anything.

Roger. Humph!—Diggory, I do not deal in philters; they are out of date—but I know a charm will win her love.

Diggory. Tell it me for the love of—

Roger. Thou wilt betray it, Diggory.

Diggory. Never! Never!

Roger. Omit thou but a word of it, and the maiden's lost to thee—but con it well, and all her beauties will be thine.

Diggory. Oh! Doctor!

Roger. Take of the rendered grease of three black bears—do not fail in that—anoint thy curly locks—

Diggory. My hair is straight.

Roger. Never mind—but rub; and, as thou dost, repeat these words:

> *Lady love, lady love, where e'er thou be,*
> *Think of no man but only me;*
> *Love me, and wed me, and call me thine own,*
> *Ting-a-ling, ting-a-ling, ting-a-ling, Joan.*

Diggory. What is that " Ting-a-ling, ting-a-ling"?

Roger. That is the chief element of the charm—don't forget it. Having done this on nine successive days—dost thou follow me?

Diggory. Aye, sir.

Roger. On the tenth go to the barber's and have thy hair cut short.

Diggory. But, sir, my hair is my best feature!

Roger. It is with many; cut it, however, or lose the worth of all of the charm. Dost thou hear, Diggory? Cut thy hair short or never win fair woman. Farewell.

Diggory. I thank you, sir. [*Going*] " Lady love, ting-a-ling "—nay, that's not it.

Roger. Diggory!

Diggory. Yes, sir.

Roger. Who are with the Governor?

Diggory. The worthy ministers, Master Wilson and Master Dimsdell.

Roger. Very well. [*Exit Diggory, trying to recall the verse.* Ah! Diggory, thou art but a dram of love in a fluid ounce of fool! And so may we label all mankind. For instance: the Governor is a wise man and a politic; Wilson a good man and a pious; Dimsdell—ah! there I pause, for what fine formula can sum the qualities of that same Arthur Dimsdell? He's not a fool; nor mad; nor truly cataleptic—yet he's moody, falls in trance, and I suspect his power as a preacher comes from ecstasy. Something he is akin to genius—yet he hath it not, for though his aim be true enough, he often flashes in the pan when genius would have hit the mark. I'll write his case in Latin! What a study

that would be if I could first find out the reason why he
clutches at his breast!—If once I find him in a trance, alone—
ah! here they come.

Enter GOVERNOR BELLINGHAM, REV. JOHN WILSON,
REV. ARTHUR DIMSDELL, *and following them,*
with a tray of wine, DIGGORY.

Wilson. Good morrow, Doctor.
Roger. Good morning, gentlemen.
Governor. [*To Diggory.*] Leave the wine within the summer house. Good morning, Doctor. When Mistress Prynne
doth come conduct her hither.
Diggory. Sir, she's coming this way now.
Governor. Very well. Go. [*Exit Diggory.*] Doctor, we
debate what disposition should be made of Hester Prynne's
young child. We ask your aid—but here she is.

Enter HESTER PRYNNE.

Hester. Your worship hath been pleased to summon me
To bring my child before you.
Governor.   Where is the child?
Hester. The babe is sick but answers by attorney.
What is your will?
Governor.   Some pious matrons, Hester,
Have charged that thou art not a person fit
To rear that infant immortality,
And guide it unto God.
Hester.   God gave the child
In rich exchange for all things else which I,
Poor sinful I, had forfeited; and now
You, who have made yourselves the flails of God,

Would separate the wheat from chaff before
The grain is ripe, and take her from me.
Oh! ye are wise!   No doubt ye see beyond
The purpose of Almighty God who gave
The child to me!

    Governor.   Nay, take it not to heart,
For, Hester, duty to the child we owe
To put its soul upon the way that leads
To Heaven.   She will be cared for tenderly.

    Hester. She is the last small link that binds my soul
To earth, the tiny needle that doth point
My way to Heaven.   You shall not take her from me!
Speak thou for me [*To Dimsdell*]; as my pastor speak;
Speak now; and say if any harm from me
Will hurt the child.   I will not part with her!
Say if thou canst, for thou hast sympathies
Which these men lack, say what the mother's rights
Are in her child; and what those rights must be
When naught beside the child is left to her—
Her husband gone, her friends deserted,
No reputation, no sympathy, no love—
But only those twin brands of shame, her baby
And The Scarlet Letter!

    Dimsdell. I have a dual duty to discharge;
I am this woman's pastor—and her friend,
And therefore she hath called me to defend her;
I am, beside, a member of your council,
And hence am with you in your consultation;
And yet, I think, these duties may be made
To yoke and draw me to a just conclusion.

Wilson. Thou also hast a duty to the child.

Dimsdell. Aye, so I have. Our aim is well enough,
But let us pause before we do adopt
A means that varies from the one marked out
By God and Nature.

Governor.   Is there not command
To teach our children in the fear of God
And guide them from impurity?

Dimsdell. God gave us mothers when He gave us life,
And to their tender care He did entrust
The mortal and immortal parts of us.
What then? Would we improve upon His system;
Would we now deprive this little one
Of that fond mother-care which nurtures her?
Or would we put, in place of mother-love,
The cold, hard, formal training of a paid
Instructor?

Governor. But is this woman, stained with sin,
A mother to entrust a child to?

Dimsdell. That question God hath answered; and we know
The stain of sin doth fade beneath the bleach
Of true repentance; through it all appears
The woven figure of the woman-fabric—
Her motherhood!
We owe our lives to woman's suffering,
We owe our health unto her temperance,
We owe her all the best of us. Let God
Condemn her sin, but let us not presume
To punish her where He hath healed her heart.

Wilson. There is weight in what he says.

Roger. Yea, and earnestness!

Governor. Well, Hester, go thy way; the child is thine.
Remember thou dost owe a gentle thanks
Unto this pious man. Go, Hester, keep
The child. Think well upon his words; be thou
A mother in all righteousness, as well
As in thy sin. Farewell.

Hester. I thank you, gentlemen. [*Exit.*

Wilson. That woman would have been a noble wife
Had not some villain robbed her of her dower.

Governor. Come, gentlemen, this business well is ended,
And, Dimsdell, yours is all the credit of it;
For one I thank you.

Roger. We all do thank you, sir.

Governor. Come, let us drain a cup of wine; and then
Go in.

Dimsdell. I beg you to excuse me.

Roger. And me,
I pray. I'll stay with Dimsdell.

Governor. Well, Wilson, you
Shall not escape me. Gentlemen, the wine
We leave you; keep it company.—And, Dimsdell,
Forget it not, to-morrow thou must preach
A grand election sermon. The people do
Expect a master effort, man. Fail not.

[*Exeunt Governor and Wilson.*

Roger. He will not fail them, Governor; a tongue
Of flame is his. What ails thee, Dimsdell?
How now? Why man!

Dimsdell. I'm very weak. The pain about my heart—

Roger. Nay, courage, man! 'Twill leave thee soon.
I'll get a cup of wine to cheer thee up.

Dimsdell. Do, I pray. And, Doctor, give me something
to abate this agony.

Roger. I will.   [*Exit.*

Dimsdell. Try how I may, there's no escape from pain.
I robbed the law's strong arm, and thereby put
The lash in conscience' hand—and yet I thought
Hypocrisy a duty to my calling!
'Twere better I were known as what I am,
Than still to hide my sin beneath the garb
Of outward purity! 'Twere better now,
By Hester's side, to bear opprobrium,
And brave what man may do, than still to nurse
This misery in secret!

Re-enter ROGER *with wine-tray; places it upon a bench and,
taking a vial from a pocket medicine-case, pours a few drops
into a wine-glass, then fills the glass with wine.*

Roger. A minim more would lull him into sleep.
Here is the chance—and here the will—to learn
His secret malady. What holds me back?
Conscience? Tut, tut! It will not harm him!
'Twill do him good to sleep; 'twill do me good
To know the why he clutches at his breast.
I'll do it.   [*Pours more from vial.*
Sir, drink this off.

Dimsdell. I thank thee, kind physician.   [*Drinks.*

Roger. Nay, thank me not. Now, take a glass of wine.
                              [*Giving him another glass.*

Dimsdell. Methinks, the wine is richer than is common.
Roger. Thirst always gives an added age to wine.
This is right Xeres.   Hast been in Spain?
Dimsdell. Nay, but the wine hath.   I feel its warmth.
Roger. Truly, it is a grand inquisitor;
'Twill search each petty heresy that taints
Thy blood, and burn it to a cinder.
Dimsdell. How many leagues it came to serve my need.
Roger. Aye, a thousand, and a thousand more!
Dimsdell. I would not go so far for it just now,
For through my limbs there creeps a lang'rous ease
Like that which doth precede deep slumber.
Roger. Rest here upon this bench.   [*Dimsdell sits, half*
Give way unto your drowsiness; it is   *reclining.*
Not sleep, but rest and relaxation.   There!
I'll keep you company.
Dimsdell. Do.
Roger. [*Pouring wine and drinking.*] This wine is liquid gold.
I quaff to your good health and ease of mind.
This is good wine.   It warms my chilly blood
With all the dreamy heat of Spain.   I hear
The clack of th' castinet and th' droning twang
Of stringéd instruments; while there before
Mine eyes brown, yielding beauties dance in time
To the pulsing music of a saraband!
And yet there is a flavor of the sea,   [*Sipping wine.*
The long-drawn heaving of the ocean wave,
The gentle cradling of a tropic tide;
Its native golden sun—I fear you sleep?
Or do the travels of the wine so rock

Your soul that self is lost in revery?
Why, man, dream not too much of placid bliss;
Nor wine, nor man, can reach this clear perfection
Until they pass the rack of thunder and
Of hurricane.—'Tis on us now! Awake! [*Shouting in Dims-*
My friend, awake! Dost thou not hear the storm? *dell's ear.*
Oh! how it shrieks and whistles through the shrouds!
The awful guns of heaven boom in our ears—
Nay, that was the mainsail gone by the board,
Flapping with cannon roar.
You do not follow me. O, come, I say!
This is no sermon. You cannot be asleep,
Yet feign you are to cheat me of my story.
Wake up, my friend. You carry the jest too far.

      Roger cautiously shakes Dimsdell.

So soon! So sound!   [*Looks around.*
I fear you are not easy; thus. That's better.
Your pardon, sir, your collar's much too tight.
Now will I steal his hidden mystery,
And learn the secret of his lengthened pain;
Cure him and gain great honor. To think a man
Would case himself in buttons like an armour!
Now, shirt——
Merciful God! what miracle is this!
A stigma! Aye! a stigma! the letter "A"
In blood suffused! The counterpart of that
Which Hester wears, but palpitating here
In life! This is beyond my skill.
Ah! David! David! Thou art the man! Thou wouldst
Have set me in the hot forefront of battle

Hadst thou but known me as Uriah!
Bah!
Why, what a brainless dullard have I been,
To see this pretty puff-ball of a preacher
Wax large before mine eyes in righteous husk—
And think him whole within—when but a touch,
But one, had aired his rottenness!
Oh! dotard that I am! blind, deaf and stupid!
It takes a miracle to make me see
What lay before me open.   He did take
Her part; ever professed himself her friend;
And at her trial fell in trance.   What more?
He is the man!   He is the man!
Now ends our game of hoodman blind; oh, I
Was warm, so very warm at times, so hot,
Did almost touch thee; yet I knew thee not
For him I sought.   Thou cunning hypocrite!
It must be I am fitted to my state,
Dull, trusting and incapable;
Or else—why surely I'm a fool.—
Had I been here when Hester bore her child,
I would have fondly dreamed it was mine own;
Put on the unearned pride that old men wear
When their young wives bear children.
A pretty baby, sir!   My grandchild?—No;
Mine own; my very own!   Nay, wrong me not;
I'm not so old—not so damned old after all!
A ghe! a ghoo!   Are not the eyes like mine?—
Yea, would have dandled it upon my knee,
And coddled each succeeding drop, as though

My fires had distilled them.
But—now I know—my knowledge must be hid.
Back shirt! cover blazoned infamy
And let the whited front still hide from man
The sepulchre of crime that festers here.
He will not wake within an hour. I'll go
Inform the Governor he sleeps, and have
Him order none disturb his pious rest.
Then I'll return and calmly probe his soul.
Sleep on! Sleep on! *[Exit Roger.*

SCENE II.—*Another part of the garden.* *Enter alone,* DIG-
GORY.

Diggory. If there be no true charm but it hath a touch of
folly in it, this one must be most potent. Now a wise man
would not think there's that virtue in a bit of grease, a
jingling rhyme, and a hair cut, that one might thereby win
a woman's love—but the wise are fools in love. I have here
the lard of three bears—one more than the old adage of
" bear and forbear "—and with it I am to anoint my head
as an enchantment to bring about my marriage to Betsey—
marry, I'll temper the strength of the charm with a little
bergamot, for in truth two of the bears have been dead over-
long. Whew!—Aha! enchantment is the only highway to
success in love! Now let me see: " Lady love, lady love,
where'er you be "—

Betsey. [*Singing behind the scenes*]

> *Little bird, little bird, come tell me true;*
> *If I love my love, as your love loves you,*
> *And if he loves me, as you love your mate;*
> *How long, little bird, should I make him wait?*

Diggory. That's Betsey singing now! If the charm works like this, bear fat will be worth its weight in gold. But perhaps my features may have pleased her after all—I'm not bad to look upon; and truly I would save my hair; it's the best part about me. Singing again.

Betsey. [*Singing behind the scenes*]·

> *In Summer-tide, sweet Summer-tide,*
> *O, what can a maiden do,*
> *If, while he walks close by her side,*
> *Her lover begins to woo ?*

Diggory. Now I wonder where she learnt all those pro-fane songs? From some liberal folk in the old country, no doubt; they ill become a puritan. If she were a little slower in her speech, what an angel she would be! As it is, she is a very good woman, tongue and all.

Betsey. [*Singing again, behind the scenes.*]

> *For her, of buttercups and violets,*
> *A circlet for her hair he makes ;*
> *And sings, in roundelays and triolets,*
> *A song that soon her fancy takes.*
> *In Summer-tide, sweet Summer-tide,*
> *O, what can a maiden do,*
> *If, while he walks close by her side,*
> *Her lover begins to woo ?*

Diggory. I'm not a judge of songs, but if she means half she says—and a woman sometimes does—some one is about to be the top feather in Fortune's cap; it may be me. I'll try my luck once more. [*Going toward R. wing*] Why, here she comes.

Enter BETSEY, *with a pair of butter paddles.*

Betsey. [*Entering.*]

> *Adown the moonlit path they walk,*
> *Through all the world called lover's lane,*
> *And hand in hand they sigh and talk*
> *Of the love that binds them, happy twain!*

What are you gaping like a great gaby for?

Diggory. For Fortune to drop the plum into my mouth.

Betsey. Where is the plum?

Diggory. There. [*Pointing at her.*]

Betsey. You silly fellow! yesterday I was a peach; the day before strawberries and cream; the day before that a rose; and last week a dove—marry, I don't coo for you! Can I be all these things at once and still be Betsey Tomkins?

Diggory. O, Betsey, thou art all the world to me!

Betsey. O, Diggory, thou art a great fool to me! Why, man, thy head is as soft as a pat of butter; I could take it between my paddles, like this, and mold it into any shape I chose.

Diggory. So you may, Betsey; so you may. And, Betsey, for the love of mercy, mold it into the head of thy future husband.

Betsey. 'Twould take a pair of shears to do that.

Diggory. Wouldst thou marry me, Betsey, if I should lose my pretty locks?

Betsey. I would not marry you with them, that's flat.

Diggory. Shall I shave my head or only clip it close?

Betsey. Cut it off, Diggory, cut it off.

Diggory. Kiss me but once, Betsey, and I'll cut my head

off; 'tis of little use to me now, and if thou dost marry me—
well, thy head shall rest upon my shoulder, like this, and
one head is enough for any pair of shoulders.

Betsey.   *In Summer-tide, sweet Summer-tide,*
                O, what can a maiden do, etc.   [*Exeunt.*

SCENE III.—*The same as in Scene I of this act.   Dimsdell
asleep upon a garden bench, half reclining.   Enter* ROGER
PRYNNE, *called Chillingworth.*

Roger. To kill were easy; aye, but—to stretch his life
As on a rack—were that not better still?
Dead, I'd bury with him my revenge;
But while he lives the old account will stand
At daily usury.
I'll tent his agony, prolong it here,
Even here where I may feed upon it;
Not send him hence beyond my reach.   Aye!
I'll fight with death to keep him for mine own.
But, now—
O, I must calm myself or miss my aim!
For, like a hunter when first he sees the buck,
My nerves are all unstrung.   This weakling trick
Of overearnestness betrays the fool
In me; and yet we know it, though we profit not,
The eager hand doth ever spill the cup
That lifted carefully would quench our thirst.
I must assume a wise placidity;
As he puts on—Ah! damnéd hypocrite!—
The air of purity. (*Approaches Dimsdell.*)
I'll drink dissimulation at the source;

I'll study him.—Thus might an angel look
When, wearied with the music of the spheres,
He laid him down upon a roseate bank
To dream of holiness!—He hath not stirred.—
'Twas well I did not speak to Bellingham,
For we have not been noted.   Good, so far.
All eyes are busy with their own affairs ;
I'll wake him now and foil discovery.

Takes vial from pocket medicine case.

Our native drugs are balanced well ; one plant
Sucks in the beams the sleepy moon sends down,
Another drinks the waking draught of dawn.
That made him sleep, but this—Ah !
A mouldy mummied corse that in the tomb
A thousand years had lain, would wake once more,
If but three drops of this should touch its lips.
I'll give you, sir, but two.

Drops liquid into glass and fills with wine.
                              There, swallow it.
Administering to Dimsdell.

Now, let me see—he must not know how long
He slept,—and by the sun it is not long—
I have't ; I'll make him think he merely lost
Himself while I was talking.

*Dimsdell stirs.   Roger pours a glass of wine and takes position
he occupied when Dimsdell fell asleep.   Speaks as
in continuation of former speech.*
                              Mellow wine

Is Nature's golden bounty unto man.
And it hath well been said: Dame Nature is
A gentle mother if we follow her;
But if she drives our steps no fury wields
A fiercer lash ; yet all her punishments
Are kindly meant; our puny faculties
Would nest forever fledgeling in our minds,
Did not her wise austerity compel
Their flight.

*Dimsdell wakes with a start and recovers himself as one who
would not seem rude.*

          Or, put the same in other words:
That man is noble who doth fear no fate
Which may afflict humanity; but, like
A gallant soldier, meets the charge half way,
And takes his wounds a-jesting.
Now ev'ry one of us, whom Nature whips,
Must take it meekly; for she means our good;
And learn to go along with her.
    Dimsdell.   I fear
I dozed and lost the thread of argument.
I pray you, pardon me.
    Roger.   I did not note it.
But, be it so, come sun yourself; drive out
The fog and vapor that becloud your mind,
And let the warmth of nature take their place.
Nature retrieves our losses, or charges them
Against us; all things do rest, even the plants
Do slumber as they grow.
    Dimsdell.   How greedily

The flow'rs drink up the wine our golden sun
Pours down on them, yet blush to own their drinking!
   Roger. This is the New World, man; and Nature here
Is lusty; drink in thy dole of heat and light;
For even I, drenched in the golden rain,
Feel pulsings of lost paradise that make
My blood leap with th' quick-step bound of youth.
This is the very show'r of gold in which
Jove comes to fill the longing world with life.
And as he kisses her with ling'ring lips,
All Nature lies wide open to th' warm embrace
And quickens in his arms.—All, all, but thou!
For thou art single as the northern pole;
As cold, as distant, and unreachable
To what hath passion's warmth; and, though
Thy life be at its summer solstice—bright
With day—thy heart still turns to barren ice,
More bleak than many a wintry age.
   Dimsdell. How can I change my disposition, Doctor?
   Roger. Widen the thin ecliptic of thy life;
Revolve upon another axis, man ;
Let love, the sun of life, beam meltingly
Upon thy heart and thaw it into happiness.
Marry, man, marry.
   Dimsdell. I cannot marry: I have my work to do.
   Roger. If work precedent were to love, the world
Would be unpeopled. This is the month of June,
And now the locust and the linden tree
Do wed the zephyrs as they blow, and weight
The air with oversweetness.—What song is that?

[Voice of Betsey singing behind scenes.]

For her, of buttercups and violets,
*   A circlet for her hair he makes;*
And sings, in roundelays and triolets,
*   A song that soon her fancy takes.*
In Summer-tide, sweet Summer-tide,
*   O, what can a maiden do,*
If, while he walks close by her side,
*   Her lover begins to woo?*

Roger. That maid is innocent and happy too.
You may have noticed that—when the heart
Is pure—love overflows the lips in song
As sweet and limpid as a mountain spring;
But—when it's bitter with base treachery—
It dams itself against all utterance,
And either mines the soul, or, breaking forth,
Sweeps downward to destruction. Oh! 'tis true,
Love is the lyric happiness of youth;
And they, who sing its perfect melody,
Do from the honest parish register
Still take their tune. And so must you. For you
Are now in the very period of youth
When myriads of unborn beings knock loud and long
Upon the willing portals of the heart
For entrance into life. Deny it not;
I say but truth—I once was young myself.
Behold the means!

Enter MARTHA WILSON, *carrying a bunch of roses.*

Dimsdell. Oh! Oh! *[Clasps his breast.]*

Roger. Whither so fast, Martha, that thou canst not speak to us?

Martha. Oh! I beg your pardon, Doctor. Good morning, sir. I seek my father; is he with the Governor?

Roger. Knowledge is costly, Martha; yet thou art rich enough to buy more than information. For one of those sweet roses, I'll tell you he is well and with the Governor.

Martha. You beg it prettily. [*Giving Roger a rose.*

Roger. Pure and fragrant as the giver—marry, the blush becomes it not so well; it does not come and go. Martha, thy father and the Governor are in the library. Is that not worth another rose?

Martha. Nay, only a very little one; for when he talks of books he's always loath to come with me.

Roger. Nay, slander him not. But, Martha, books or no books, for two more roses I will bring him here; and, truly, fathers were cheap at three roses apiece. What say you?

Martha. Nay, I'll go myself; but do not think I grudge the roses; here they are. You have not begged of me [*To Dimsdell*]. May I beg you to accept this? Gentlemen, farewell. [*Exit Martha.*

Roger. Roses, and you asked her not!
In love! in love! up to the eyes in love!
She'll drown in love unless you marry her!

Dimsdell. Oh! that I were worthy of her!

Roger. Dost love her, Dimsdell? Ah! she's worthy love.
She's fair and young; of gentle birth and rich;
And warm and pure and spirit-like as flame
That floats above new brandy.

Dimsdell. Out upon thee, satyr! Thou dishonorest her.

Roger. Not a whit. Is't dishonor to her purity
To urge thy smoky flame to brightness worthy
Of her? 'Tis what she wishes most; witness
Her confusion and her telltale blushes.
Do me justice, man; my thoughts are pure
And dwell on lawful marriage only.   Thou, thou
Alone, couldst see impurity in that.
I spoke of thee, man, of thee; and who
Beside thyself would think a mottled thought
Could touch a maiden linked to thee in words
Or fact?
     Dimsdell. Oh! Oh!   [*Clutching at his breast.*
     Roger. Had I young daughters by the score, each fair
As Hebe, as voluptuous as Venus,
All thinly clad as in the golden age,
I could not wish a chaster keeper of them.
Nay, had I wives in droves like Solomon,
I'd make thee Kislah Aga of my harem,
Chief eunuch and sole security—What!
Call me satyr when I urge in bounds
The boundless beauties of pure maidenhood,
And bid thee wed them!   Thus best advices are
Construed amiss, and what we kindly mean
Turned into scorn and filthiness!
     Dimsdell. Forgive me, Doctor; I'm ill at ease.   This pain
Is like a stick thrust in a spring; it muddies
All my thoughts. Oh! Oh! [*Pressing his hands to his breast.*
     Roger. Come, Dimsdell, listen to a bit of reason.
Thy body is as sound as a red apple
In November.   The pain's imaginary.

Marry, man, marry; thy wife will prove
A counter-irritant and drive the pain away.

    Dimsdell. No more of that, I pray you.

    Roger. Not enough of it, not enough of it!

    Dimsdell. No more, no more! I must not marry.

    Roger. Think once again, man; if that thy mind
Can pardon the suggestion—and, mark, I urge it
With all diffidence—there is a way,
Wherein the low opinion thou doth hold
Of thine own virtues—not held by any else—
May wed with beauty all unspeakable,
Raise up a noble lady, and show thy christian
Spirit to the world.

    Dimsdell. And what is that?

    Roger.   Wed Hester Prynne.

    Dimsdell. Wed Hester Prynne?

    Roger.   Aye! 'twas that I said.
She is a paragon—nay, beauty's self.
All other women are but kitchen-maids
Beside her loveliness.

    Dimsdell. Wed Hester Prynne!

    Roger. I hear her husband left her well to do;
And as for that small blot that sullies her
'Twill fade when covered by thy name.

    Dimsdell. Hester Prynne!

    Roger. What act more merciful, more christianlike?
Redeem the reputation of her child,
And to the jeers of fools stop up thine ears;
Enwrap thee in her gentle arms, lay down
Thine aching head upon her tender breast,

And dream thyself in paradise.

   Dimsdell. Thou fiend of Hell!   I know thee now; thou
But once in thine own form, and ever since   [cam'st
Hast been too near me in a worser one.
Back to the pit, I say!   No more of tempting!

   Roger. Art mad?   I'm man as thou dost seem to be;
I'm not a fiend.

   Dimsdell. What dost thou know?   [*Shaking Roger by the*

   Roger. Only this—thou art as cowardly   *shoulders.*
As thou art lecherous.   What! betray
A woman!   Desert her in her misery!
Refuse to marry her!
And all the while, cloaked in thy ministry,
Dispense the sacraments of God to children—
How canst thou do it?

   Dimsdell. If thou be not Satan, why raise this cloud?
Why vanish from my sight?   Yet I did touch him even now—
I'll kill him—Kill, kill, kill—now, now, now—

   Roger. In trance again!   Help!   Help!   Help!

*Dimsdell becomes rigid ; with arm uplifted as if to strike a death
    blow.   His speech thickens, and he stands motionless.
             Roger supports him.*

ACT IV.

SCENE I.—*A room.* DIMSDELL *upon a couch in a cataleptic trance.* ROGER PRYNNE *watching him. Two chairs; other furniture heavy and immovable.*

Roger. [*Feeling Dimsdell's pulse*] There's been no change.
A very long trance.
At times he mumbles; at other times, as now,
He lies like death. · If ev'ry murderer
Were stricken with the image of the thing
Which he would deal, 'twould be a blessing! Yet
When consciousness returns, with it will come
The murderous disposition; for in these cases
The mind, although it wanders while the trance
Is on, always comes back upon its path
Where first it left it. Therefore, 'twere wise in me
To be on guard. Well, so I am; but what—
What fear should drive me hence, or make me leave
The study of his case? He hath no arms
But such as both of us were born with;
And despite my age I am his equal that way.
Ah! a chair swung by a furious man
Might make an omelet of my brain;
Therefore, one chair will do—and that for me. [*Removes chair.*

Enter GOVERNOR BELLINGHAM *in robes of office.*

Governor. Good morning, Doctor.

Roger. Good morning, Governor. I wish you, sir,
As happy and as prosperous a term
In office, as that just closing.

Governor.   I thank you, sir.
Has Dimsdell recovered from his trance?

Roger. Not yet.   There he lies.

Governor.   Wonderful!
Can you account for his condition, Doctor?

Roger. There's no accounting for it, Governor.
This is the second trance I've seen him in;
How many more he's had, God only knows.

Governor. 'Tis most unfortunate that we must lack
His eloquence to-day.   The people, who
Always love high-sounding words more than
Wise thoughts, prefer the music of his voice
To good old Wilson's drone.   Why isn't he in bed?

Roger. Oh! there are many reasons; 'twould take too long
To tell you now; but at another time
I'll ask your patience for a tale more strange
Than ever made your flesh to creep.

Governor. Is there mystery in the case?

Roger. Mystery! aye, and miracle, too!
You know him, Governor—a man whose nerves
Are gossamers, too fine to sift the music
Of the blasts that blow about our burly world,
And only fit for harps whereon Zephyrus
In Elysium might breathe.—And yet this man—
Oh! you'd not believe it if I told you.

Enter Servant.

Servant. Your worship is asked for at the door.

Governor. Say I am coming. We'll speak again of this.

[*Exit Servant.*

I must be gone. We servants of the State
Are slaves to show, and serve the people best
When most we trick them. The pageant of the day
Goes much against my better judgment, but
The crowd will have it so, and so farewell.

Roger. One moment, if you please. If he revives
He'll pick the thread of life up where he dropt it;
He may desire to preach, as he hath promised you,
And, if he doth, 'twere better not to thwart him.

Governor. Very well. I'll speak to Wilson.

Roger. I'm sorry I cannot go with you. Farewell.

Exit Governor. Dimsdell moves. Roger goes to his side and examines him.

The pulse hath quickened. He moves his lips.

Dimsdell mumbles indistinctly.

I cannot catch it.—

Dimsdell. Think of it no more, my love.—
Our troubles now are ended, Hester;
The gentle current of our mingled lives,
Long parted by the barren, rocky isle
Of hard necessity, flows reunited on.

Roger. Indeed!

Dimsdell. How sweet it is, in the afternoon of life,
To walk thus, hand in hand, Hester. And as

The golden sun of love falls gently down
Into the purple glory of the West,
We'll follow it.

    Roger.   A lengthy jump—from sinning youth
Plump into the middle of an honored age!
Yet thus the mind, in trance or dream, achieves
Without an effort what it wills.   Again?

    Dimsdell. Sir, take my daughter and my blessing, too;
Cherish her as the apple of thine eye;
Still shield her from the buffets of the world;
Let thy tenderness breathe gentle love
Like an Italian air sung at twilight,
When the melody without tunes that within
Until the soul arising on the wings
Of music soars into Heaven.

    Roger. Is there nothing in heredity? Or will
The orange-blossom take its fragrance from
The Heaven above; its origin forgot?

    Dimsdell. Hester, although the snow upon thy head
Be white as that on yonder distant mount,
Thine eyes are blue and deep as Leman's lake
That lies before us.

    Roger. Thus in our dreams we picture what we wish;
Not held to time or place; and while the body,
Like an anchor, sinks in mud, the wingéd craft
Swings with the tide of thought.
He's in Geneva now; Hester with him;
His daughter honorably married;
And all the pains of yesterday forgot.
I'll write it down.   *[Roger makes notes.*

Dimsdell. Good night, dear wife, good night.
The stars of Heaven melt into angel forms
Which stoop to lift me to the gates of bliss.
Farewell, farewell! Nay, weep not, Hester;
Our sins are now forgiven.
Yea, though I walk through the valley of th' shadow of death,
I will fear no evil.—Say it with me, Hester.
   Roger. Will he die thus?   [*Examines Dimsdell.*
The pulse is weak—a clammy sweat—
'Tis but the culmination of the trance.
'Tis but a dream. A dream! Yet one must die;
And to our human thought that death were best
That came preceded by a flag of truce
To parley peace. To pass away In dreams—
Without the vain regret for work undone;
Without a load of sin to weight the soul;
With all the argentry of honored age
To frost our past; with all the fiercer heats
Of life burnt out into the cold, gray ash—
That were peace! Then might a man yield up
The willing ghost as calmly as a child
That falls asleep upon its mother's breast
To wake in paradise.

           Dimsdell starts up.

   Dimsdell. I see thee now—and now I'll kill, kill, kill—
If thou be Satan I cannot harm thee—
But if a man—

*Dimsdell attempts to reach Roger, who keeps the one chair of the
room in front of him and thus wards off Dimsdell.*

Roger. Madman, listen! Thou canst not harm me, yet I am not Satan. My name is Roger Prynne. I am the husband of the woman you have wronged.

Dimsdell. Thou Roger Prynne?

Roger. Aye, Roger Prynne and thine accuser.

Dimsdell looks about the room as though dazed.

Dimsdell. Why, how is this?—But now, the Governor's garden—and now, my room!—But now, just now, old Doctor Chillingworth—and now, mine enemy, Roger Prynne! Thou art the Devil himself!—Thou shalt not trick me thus.

Band music in distance.

Roger. Trick thee? Why, madman, thou hast been in trance since yester noon. Trick thee! I like the word! 'Tis now the time of day when thou shouldst preach the great Election Sermon, the one event that makes or mars you preachers. Dost hear the music? A day hath passed since thou wast in the garden. They are marching even now to the market place.

Dimsdell. What shall I do?   [*Aloud, but to himself.*

Roger. Do? Stay here and settle our account; or else go on and publish thyself as what thou art—a hypocrite.

Dimsdell. I see it now! — Ah! Satan! Satan!—thou wouldst affright my soul and make me lose my well earned honors. Why, Roger Prynne is dead—dead. 'Twas told on good report two years ago. And now—oh! try it if thou wilt—I'll have thee burnt, burnt—burnt at the stake, if thou accusest me! Who would believe thee? Stand aside, I say! Let me pass!

Roger. How came the stigma on thy breast?

Dimsdell. Thou knowest!—Make way, I tell thee!—Thou didst place it there!—Make way!

They struggle. Roger interposes the chair between himself and Dimsdell. Finally, Dimsdell wrenches the chair from Roger, flings it aside, and, grappling him, chokes Roger to death.

Dimsdell. [*Panting*] A man! A man! A man!—Dead! dead! dead!—Nay—like a man!—Like a dead man!—A trick!—A devilish trick!—Did he not come in angel form —and then as Doctor Chillingworth—and then as Roger Prynne—and now,—and now, as a dead body?

Spurning Roger with his foot.

O, Devil, I'll avoid thee yet!—I'll confess my crime and thus unslip the noose about my soul!

Hurriedly prepares to depart.

He said we'd meet again! We have, and 'tis the last time! [*Exit.*

SCENE II.—*Plain curtain, down. Music. Music ceases; subdued sounds as of a multitude back of curtain. Then the voice of Dimsdell rises as quiet returns.*

Dimsdell. And now, good friends, Electors and Elected,
Although my speech hath run a lengthened course,
And what I purposed hath been said in full,
There's more comes to me now.
What is our purpose and our destiny?

Curtain rises rapidly, disclosing stage set as in Act I, Scene III. Dimsdell upon a rostrum on church steps. Militia standing at rest. Citizens and officials in gala attire.

We call us English, Anglo-Saxon;
And from the Old we come to build the New,
The equal England of our expectation.
Here in the wilderness, the first small germs
Of man's long-promised freedom find their soil;
Here hidden will they rot a little while;
Anon, the sprouts will break our troubled land,
Thrust forth the first red blades, and thence grow on,
Forever and forever!
I see this vast expanse of continent,
That dwarfs the noble states of cultured Europe,
Spread out before me like a map, from pole
To pole, and from the rising to the setting sun.
I see it teem with myriads; I see
Its densely peopled towns and villages;
I see its ports, greater than any known,
Send forth their riches to the hungry world.
I see, O blessed, wondrous sight! the strength
Of Anglo-Saxondom—our mighty England
And our great America, as one—
The Lion and the Eagle side by side,—
Leading the vanguard of humanity!
And more I see; I see the rise of man
Merely as man!
Let the day come, O Lord, when man, without
Addition to that noble title—man—
Can stand erect before his fellow-man,
Outface Oppression with his flashing eye,
And stamp and grind proud Tyranny to dust.
Put in our hearts, O, Gracious God, the yeast

Of freedom ; let it work our natures free,
Although it break to recombine again
The atoms of each state.
Send down thy pulsing tongues of burning truth ;
Fire our souls with love of human kind ;
Let hate consume itself ; let war thresh out
The brutal part of man, and fit us for
The last long period of peace.

A pause, then cries severally.

First Citizen. Is he an angel or a man? Sure Gabriel
himself.
Second Citizen. Look! He faints.
Third Citizen. Poor minister!
Dimsdell. [*Rallying himself*] I will speak on.
Governor. My pious friend, wear not thy body out
To please our willing ears. Thou hast exceeded
Thy feeble strength already. Cease, man ;
Demosthenes himself could not have stood
The strain which thou hast undergone. Prithee,—
Dimsdell. I thank you ; reason not my wastefulness,
For, if you make me answer you, you cause
More waste. My taper's burnt already.
It flickers even now, and, ere I leave
This place, my light, my life will go.
Question me not,
For, now I have fulfilled my public function,
There hurries on a duty of a private kind
I must perform at once or not at all ;
Too long delayed already.

My friends, my life is flowing fast away,
I, that should be at full or on the turn,
Am near my lowest ebb.
This gnawing at my heart hath eaten through,
And now my soul releasing body bondage
Will take its flight—but where?
 First Citizen. It goes to Heaven when it flies;
But go not now.
 Dimsdell. Behold yon woman with The Scarlet Letter.
 Citizens. Oh, shame upon her! Fie!
 Dimsdell. Nay, shame on me; her sufferings have made
Her pure, but mine, beneath this lying robe,
Have eaten up my heart. Hypocrisy
Lie there [*Taking off gown*]. Now, while I do descend these
I leave my former life behind.   [steps
   Descends and goes toward pillory.

Come, Hester, come!
Come take my hand, although it be unworthy.
 Second Citizen. Is the man mad, my masters?
 Dimsdell. Not mad, friend, not mad; but newly sane.
Come, my victim, come; assist me up
The pillory, there let us stand together—
The woman of The Scarlet Letter,
And he who did this wrong.
 First Citizen. That holy man is mad. He an adulterer!
I'll believe it when th' Devil grows blind.
 Dimsdell. Support me, Hester.
   Dimsdell and Hester ascend pillory together.
Ho! all ye people of the Commonwealth,

Behold the man for whom you oft have sought,
The man who should have borne The Scarlet Letter;
For I am he.
If that the last words of one sinful man
May warn a multitude from sin, who knows
But that his errors tend toward good at last.
Let me not think my suffering in vain,
Or that my crime confessed will lead on others
Unto their downfall.
Behold me as I am—O, what a pang [*He clutches his breast*
Was that—a hypocritical adulterer.   *from now on.*
Oh!—aye, a base, a low adulterer!
O, God, prolong my breath for this confession !—
I wronged this woman who did fondly love me,
I did neglect her in my cowardice,
I shunned the public scorn.—
O, but a little while!—I stood not with her ;
I was a coward; and did deny my child.
Delay!   Delay!
Now I avow my crime, I do confess it,
[*Kneels*] And here I beg you friends, as I have begged
My God, forgive me.   Oh, I must be brief—
If any think that while I walked these streets
In seeming honor I lacked my punishment,
Look here.—   [*Tearing shirt open and disclosing stigma.*
O—h !
This cancer did begin to gnaw my breast
When Hester first put on The Scarlet Letter
And never since hath once abated.
    Voices. O, wonderful ! wonderful ! He faints ! Help ! Help !

Hester. Arthur! Arthur! one word for me! Only one!
Dimsdell. I must say more.   [*Falls.*
   Hester. Forgive him, Father! O, God, have mercy now;
Give him but breath to speak to me!
Arthur! Arthur!
   Dimsdell. Hester, my Hester, forgive—   [*Dies.*
   Hester. Farewell, farewell—dead, dead!
Nay, you shall not take him from me!
My breast shall be his pillow; and, that he may
Rest easy, I here cast off your Scarlet Letter.
   Governor. Captain, command your men to bear the body.

A solemn march.

THE END.

www.ingramcontent.com/pod-product-compliance
Lightning Source LLC
Chambersburg PA
CBHW032359020726
47499CB00008B/2814